Numbers Of The Imagination

Edited By Allie Jones

First published in Great Britain in 2023 by:

Young Writers
Remus House
Coltsfoot Drive
Peterborough
PE2 9BF
Telephone: 01733 890066
Website: www.youngwriters.co.uk

Book Design by Ashley Janson

Softback ISBN 978-1-80459-507-7

Printed and bound in the UK by BookPrintingUK
Website: www.bookprintinguk.com
YB0540P

FOREWORD

For our latest competition, Integer, we asked secondary school students to take inspiration from numbers in the world around them and create a story. Whether it's racing against a deadline, cracking a mysterious code, or writing about the significance of a certain date, the authors in this anthology have taken this idea and run with it, writing stories to entertain and inspire. Even the format they were challenged to write within - a mini saga, a story told in just 100 words - shows that numeric influence is all around! With infinite numbers, there are infinite possibilities...

The result is a thrilling and absorbing collection of tales written in a variety of styles, and it's a testament to the creativity of these young authors.

Here at Young Writers it's our aim to inspire the next generation and instill in them a love of creative writing, and what better way than to see their work in print? The imagination and skill within these pages show just a fraction of the writing skill of the next generation, and it's proof that we might just be achieving that aim! Congratulations to each of these fantastic authors, they should be very proud of themselves.

CONTENTS

Robert Gordon's College, Aberdeen

Robert Smyth Academy, Market Harborough

Scalby School, Newby

Solefield School, Sevenoaks

The Henry Beaufort School, Harestock

Values Academy, Stockingford

Wandsworth Hospital And Home Tuition PRU, London

THE STORIES

ONLY 30 SECONDS LEFT...

ROOM 237 WAS EMPTY...

AND THEN THERE WAS NONE...

I WAS PUBLIC ENEMY NUMBER 1...

I WAS DOWN TO MY LAST £5...

I ROLLED A 6...

IT WAS 2099...

I AM NUMBER 13...

The Assignment

"And... 1! Time is up I hope you have all completed the assignment. 42109 stand up, I am guessing you have some news to share. Right?"
My heart raced as I was called, I looked down, lifted my face, and gave my best smile. I was sitting at the back, so it made it worse.
Heads turned and followed me like a cat. I finally reached the blackboard 1, 5, 690, etc. My paper was empty.
Sweat drizzled down my face, time was *not* on my side.
"Time was ticking," she said, "you are not the only one."

Carmen Forton (12)
Bedford Greenacre Independent School, Bedford

My Nightmare About Room Number 63

The blood dripped from the ceiling. The carpet was stained. The wallpaper peeled off the wall. The cat dropped dead. That's when I realised this was the room from my nightmare. It was coming true. I just hoped I didn't turn into a number like my grandmother did so many full moons ago on the 31st of October. It's my mother's fault. If I hadn't been born on Halloween, on a full moon, at midnight, then I wouldn't have been cursed to turn into a number on my 13th birthday...

Izabella Howard
Bedford Greenacre Independent School, Bedford

#404

Hello? Is anyone there? God, I hope someone is there.
My name is Graham Moore, head scientist of the Tally Project, London. This account regards the experiment known as #404.
Experiment #404, our most recent attempt, has seemed to... fail. In response to the prototype being injected into the subject's body, the subject went rampant, destroying the lab, killing everyone. Killing Martin. Martin, my love.
#404 has not been seen since, but I cannot shake the feeling they'll find me before I find them. I fear this may be my last statement.
We'll meet again, Martin.
My resting promise.

Holly Mahaffey
Bradfield College, Bradfield

The Pocket Watch

My pocket watch cracked. The face frozen. The time, 01:25. The golden case was attached to a heavy chain in my breast pocket. The knife had smashed the glass covering the clock's face. The hands stopped ticking at exactly 01.25. They came out of nowhere, out from the darkness, like beasts hunting their prey. It was Christmas night. They had agreed peace. Just hours before, we were dancing and singing doing as much as we could to keep our spirits up. It was the cold, the mud and the loneliness that got us, not the fighting. And now this.

Fraser Ball (18)
Bradfield College, Bradfield

7 8 9

Blood splatters on the padded walls, muffling the white beneath it, my new shoes already stained red. My pupils dilate and I can barely feel my feet slamming against the hard floor, I glance behind me and for a moment my heart stops, I can make out a figure sprinting towards me. I left my glasses in 'The happy room' while working with #2 and her voices. My heart sinks as I realise who it is, I speed up. I latch onto the double doors and slam them into his face.
"Melissa, what happened?"
I turn around. "#7 ate #9."

Isabella Fenton (12)
Cefn Saeson Comprehensive School, Cimla

The Investigator

0759137. I'd been tracking him for years. Finally I had the last clue. We had to find the mysterious, relentless hacker who'd already killed 4 people. We didn't know how he'd done it. Some said through the screen. What? That was no help.
Suddenly the hacker in a black hood and mask appeared on my screen. *"Die!"* He pulled out a gun and shot at his camera so instinctively I moved my head. I felt a whizz. My hair started smoking, I turned around, I saw a bullet hole in my wall. I'd just dodged a bullet. He laughed maniacally.

Daniel Edward (14)
Garnock Community Campus, Glengarnock

The Mysterious Number

The number 07857 619*** kept calling. One time when that number called, I chose to answer. In a deep voice, he said, "I'm coming for you..." I quickly hung up so he couldn't get any information on me and that's when I heard thumping on the door, getting louder and louder each second...
I ran up to the bathroom, the only room with a lock in my house. Then I heard a tremendous bang and the door collapsed... then I heard loud stomping up the stairs. I got really scared, then it went silent...
The number called once more...

Sophie Lin (12)
Garnock Community Campus, Glengarnock

999..

I wake up to heat blazing above me, people banging on the door, people screaming, the roof crumbling on top of me, the fear towering over me about what's happening. I peel the door open and run downstairs with a beaming fire following me. Sprinting outside I see the whole street up in flames, the terror in my neighbours, children's eyes jumping out their heads, everyone trying to call 999 but every line gets hung up causing panic throughout the street. I call 101 to hear a voice deep and dark, "I finally finished you..."

Reese Barker (14)

Garnock Community Campus, Glengarnock

Deadly Number 241

I walked up to room number 241, I knocked on the door. No one answered. I tried to get in but it was locked. I shouted, *"Sophia!"* to see if she would answer but I got no answer...
I phoned the police to come and see if they could open the door for me.
The police arrived and bashed the door down, everyone came out their rooms to see what was going on. I walked in, I felt something wasn't right... I walked into the bathroom and saw something red on the wall it said: 'I'm coming for you'...

Sophie Mcguire (12)
Garnock Community Campus, Glengarnock

Tam

I was in room 842, the one next to the creepy old guy called Tam, Well that's what the town said he was, an old guy in his 80s, all I thought was he was just lonely and needed someone to talk to. But I was wrong, very wrong...
When I knocked on his door he flung open the door and welcomed me in. The apartment was dark and mysterious. He walked me to the kitchen then something inside me thought to myself that I'd better run out of the house and that something wasn't right but then...
Knock, knock...

Jayden Brown (13)
Garnock Community Campus, Glengarnock

The Mystery Room

I thought I'd found him but he escaped! All of the information led to him being in room 666. His fingerprints were on the door. All the cameras caught him walking in the room but he wasn't in there. I banged on the door, then I became impatient and kicked it down, but the room was empty and the lights were turned off...
I tried to turn them on, to my horror they were broken and so I turned on my flashlight but before I could do anything suddenly something came out the creaky floorboard and jumped at me...

Kerr Agnew (12)
Garnock Community Campus, Glengarnock

That One Day In 1999

So this terrible day started in 1999 and it was December 24th, Christmas Eve. It all started when I got a phone call. It was just someone, muffled, saying, "13." I thought in my head, *why would they say 13?* but then the same number texted me saying: 'You have 13 hours'. Then they sent me a photo of my son in room 237, in Hotel Camina.
I hurried to the room number 237 and I heard ticking - it was a bomb in the room with my son! I was screaming and ran in and got him home safely.

Harry Bingham (12)
Garnock Community Campus, Glengarnock

The Hotel Room

385 was the hotel room that was haunted. Every time someone went in they vanished into mid-air...
A couple of months later a nice couple with their child bought the hotel. January 9th 2032 was the day they moved in. A week later, the child turned 10, that's when the creepy stuff started happening.
The child went into her room, she felt a big breeze down her spine she got scared. She ran out, but it was too late... She felt a hand on her shoulder and she gave a big scream... She had vanished...

Holly Mcphee (12)
Garnock Community Campus, Glengarnock

Door 13

It was a cold silent morning, I woke up trembling as it was so cold. I wandered slowly downstairs and turned on the heating. I stepped into the kitchen to make myself my breakfast until I saw my beauty advent calendar. I strolled up to it and was about to open the 13th door until something made me stop. Something was telling me not to interact with the 13th door telling me it was cursed. Of course I didn't listen. It was probably nothing...
My hand reached out to the 13th door, I regretted it instantly.

Karina Craig (14)
Garnock Community Campus, Glengarnock

Room 666

I want to go home already. "Finally,'' I say with a sigh of relief. I look down at my key card again, making sure I have the right room. "666, this is my room." I unlock the door and throw myself onto the bed after a long day of travelling. As I start to drift off to sleep, the bed moves, making a screeching noise. It feels like someone is moving the bed from underneath. My heart skips a beat. I look down the side of the bed. I see a man's eye looking straight back at me...

Olivia Neilson (12)
Garnock Community Campus, Glengarnock

Phone Number +44 07359286***

It was a Saturday night, 7:30pm. I was driving home, the roads were empty, there were no cars in sight. I glanced up at my rearview mirror and saw a car with no lights on and I found that a bit odd since it was pitch-black. There were loads of turns in the road I was taking home and the car had been taking the same turns as me every single time. Then all of a sudden I felt my phone vibrate in my pocket, and then it happened again, someone was phoning me, +44 07359286***...

Ava Mckenna (12)
Garnock Community Campus, Glengarnock

The Time

The clock was ticking down fast. 5 minutes felt like it was moving faster but it could have just been my mind thinking these numbers. It didn't feel normal, there was so much going on I couldn't focus. It was stressing me out. I didn't know what was going on. I was stunned by how confused I was. I was just losing my mind. I couldn't focus. I didn't even know where I was going but somehow I was there in time. I had just made it in time for the interview.

Tyler Thomson (14)
Garnock Community Campus, Glengarnock

The Package

The delivery man handed me a parcel and I went to say, "This isn't for me-" but he had already vanished! So I went to see what it was and I opened it...
In the box was a lot of no. 4s typed over and over again on 100s of sheets of paper. (The no. 4 is bad luck in China and when you see a no. 4 you get bad luck for 10 years!)
There was a note with it. It read: 'Ha ha ha! Now you have bad luck for 10 years!'
I was so scared I fainted!

Daniel Barron-Wardrop (12)
Garnock Community Campus, Glengarnock

The Best Holiday Ever

Only 30 seconds left until school ends for the holidays. I am going to Flamingoland and I am going to lots of skate parks and waterparks. It is going to be so fun! I hope I don't get into too much trouble 'cause this is going to be the best year of my life. I am going to stay at Flamingoland first then I am going to the waterpark. Next, I am going to a skatepark and then back home. I will miss this year so much but am hoping next year it will be the best ever!

Kenzie Mcfarlane (13)
Garnock Community Campus, Glengarnock

Friday The 13th

It was Friday the 13th, 2000. It was a quiet, normal, casual day at school and I asked to go to the bathroom and as I was walking, I heard a horrendous scream. I ran into a bathroom stall and stayed quiet as there were more and more screams and I ran. I was feeling so many different emotions and then I heard a huge bang. It sounded like a gunshot so I tried to stay calm. It was extremely traumatic. Friday the 13th may be unlucky for some and it sure was for me...

Carla Murray (12)
Garnock Community Campus, Glengarnock

The Evil Granny

It was half 6 at night and Granny was getting ready for bed and I walked in to say goodnight. She made me a cup of tea and started talking about a cat called Sally who'd died 6 months ago. I was about to go and I smelled a weird smell and I asked Granny what it was. She said it was old food but I went to investigate... I went into a wardrobe and a man was hanging by a meat hook. I looked at my granny. She was holding a knife and I ran away...

Andrew Mackenzie (14)
Garnock Community Campus, Glengarnock

Left For Mercy

I looked down, my hands covered in blood. 83 was the amount of people's blood on my hands.
"Their screams, begging you to stop," teased Isaac.
I punched him in the face.
"Dammit, you're weak," Isaac cried out.
"Shut. Up!" I shouted, pointing my gun at him. I would pull the trigger, but I didn't want to, he was my brother.
"Pull the trigger," Isaac hissed, his face covered in blood. I hesitated. "Oh! Are you scar-"
I pulled the trigger.
I looked down, my hands covered in blood. 84 was the amount of people's blood on my hands.

Oana Ortan (14)
Hertswood Academy, Borehamwood

Her 12th Birthday

When the clock struck 12:12, the girl jumped under her bed, frightened, knowing that her life was minutes to its end. The night of her 12th birthday was the night she dreaded the most. All her aunties and cousins and even her mum had gone through the same thing, so she wasn't shocked, just scared. You see, 110 years ago, her great-great-grandfather killed someone, brutally, on the 12th of December 1912, 12-12-12. It'd been terrorising her family ever since. But it never leaves. It hides out in a place nobody knows - counting down the months until the next 12.

Amelia Kowalczyk (11)
Hertswood Academy, Borehamwood

13

13's my favourite number - it always has been. I was born on the 13th, my favourite time of day is 13:00. My favourite room in my house is no. 13. The worn-down bookshelves, the rotting, colourless covers of the books. The Victorian tea set always placed upon the same dainty table with metal chairs and velvet pillows. The little girl with her large brown eyes that always sits with me to drink the rich brown liquid. A splash of milk, two sugars, like always. She never says hi. Did I forget to mention? I died at 13, too.

Chloe Whitmill (13)
Hertswood Academy, Borehamwood

House 69

It was 6am in the morning. I was with 6 of my friends. One of my friends, Niki, said, "Guys, let's go to house 69. I heard that paranormal things happened there." We said okay. We went into the house and the walls were covered with 69. We split up... 6 minutes later I heard a scream! My friend Dome was behind me; the next second I heard more screams of terror and 6 bangs. As I turned around to look, Dome collapsed on the floor - behind him, Niki with a bloody gun.
We did this...

Brigitta Nemeti (13)
Hertswood Academy, Borehamwood

Numbers

I am back, back in my gory past. Vietnam again. How did I get here and what are the numbers being screamed? 735184... Where am I? Am I crazy? One second I'm on a battlefield, now I'm in an interrogation room.
A voice speaks. "Alex, you need to remember the numbers. You're the key to stopping Nova 13, deactivating the launch."
Suddenly I'm in prison. Volkov and Sterner. Volkov says, "42021."
My consciousness is back in the room. I tell the figure, "42021."
He replies in a Russian accent, "Now Europe will be poisoned, and America will be blamed."

Billy Devine (12)
Hinde House 3-16 School, Sheffield

The Keypad Killer

I watched crime documentaries, hoping to find something. I'd been on this case for months with no lead. It didn't make sense. I'd watched all the cases... except 1. 'Keypad Case - Ryan Myers'. A murderer left clues through integers. His name was on the keypad. Pathetic. I had no alternative.
Okay, 1st victim - killed March, Saturday 7th 1:55pm. D, R...
2nd victim, killed March, Thursday 30th, midnight. D, E? No! E, L. No word?
Today. No confirmed time of death. I joined the letters and... something odd.
They spelled 'Dr Eli'. But he'd just left the agency yesterday...

Ola Elbasher (12)
Hinde House 3-16 School, Sheffield

My Last Breath

2099 arrived. Still standing on this spinning orb we once called home, is me, the last woman alive. We devoured their love. Eventually the term 'we' switched to 'I'.
I was running under my own steam. I pondered, *why continue? They're going to hunt me down*. Then the realisation hit me; PTSD pins me into a hollow grave. The alarm of the mass extinction, souls of innocent women. I found myself on a cliff. I couldn't overturn them. My soul glided through the wind's last breath whilst tied with mine. We could've prevented it. But I'm just a woman, right?

Mina Ingrams (14)
Hinde House 3-16 School, Sheffield

Peace Hack

The police, they must be here for me. Scientist's invention, they can have it, but I will not be stopped. I will be the first to upload myself to the metaverse, and I will have internal peace. Suddenly I hear them raid the laboratory. I prepare by grabbing my handgun and running to the back of the room. Whatever. What they don't know is that I've planted C4 on the door. Swiftly, I detonate the bombs as soon as I hear footsteps at the door. *Boom!* They're all gone. I rush to use the machine.
79108631000985798151742086001110674206921... Finally, peace.

Zak Lindley (12)
Hinde House 3-16 School, Sheffield

The Death Counter

One more down, another life wasted. A cold breeze brushed past my face, plummeting my heart to the depths of my stomach. The death counter was the worst thing to happen under the torturous government of The Organisation.
The numbers scared us, kept us hoping for anything better, kept us from daring to do anything to free ourselves from oppression.
I used to dare to dream, my eyes closed, imagining a land where all was one and one was all. But now, sitting in this appallingly revolting cell, awaiting my execution I realised I was one against all.

Chiamaka Amadi (16)
Hinde House 3-16 School, Sheffield

The Demon Of The Tails

Red, gigantic, 100 tails - it was all a myth until 2055, when it ambushed the reality of life. It did the same thing at the start of the world. Two demons created the world.
I was walking, then I saw my friends, Rachel, and Daffodil.
We started to walk when 30 seconds later I was writhing in agony.
My eyes grew hot, and I could feel my bones snap as I began to change.
"D-d-demon!" my friend Rachel gasped, pointing at me.
My friends turned to run, but before they could escape, I ran after them with gnashing teeth...

Aaron Armstrong (13)
Hinde House 3-16 School, Sheffield

The Lottery

It's day 237. I still haven't been part of the lucky few to be chosen. Nobody knows where they go. All we know is that they go somewhere special. At least that's what I've been told. Many people have tried to sneak out, but the building is like a maze. People that come in never get out.
"Return to your rooms and remember, there is always tomorrow," said the leader. I was talking to my friends on the way to my room when suddenly I heard screams. Screams from a little girl. Then the lockdown began...

Hiba Khan (11)
Hinde House 3-16 School, Sheffield

My Name Is 7A

It's 2451. I live in a dorm with 7B and 7C. I wake up at 5:30, shower and dress. 6am, breakfast. 6:15am, bag. 6:25am, go to room 362. 6:30am, class. My efforts are futile. The school is divided into girls' and boys' quarters. There are 24 people in each room. We can't go out of the school.
7B and 7C arrive late. Shortly after that, the teacher announces, "7B and 7C, go to Office 4 - the principal's." They never return. What is happening? Seems I have to take matters into my own hands...

Oluwanifemi Adekunle (13)
Hinde House 3-16 School, Sheffield

The Numbering

I hated my daughter from the day she was born. She was no blessing. She was a curse.
The 'Number 1'...
She was the sought-out number 'royalty' you could say. But I couldn't kill her. It would feel wrong. Yet, there was only one way I could obtain my desired status.
So, I left her. Alone. 2 and a half months old, unable to sit up by herself. I hoped an animal would take her. I hoped it wouldn't count as my fault.
I misplaced my hopes again... as I am now crowned 'Number 1'...

Nomignan Kamara (16)
Hinde House 3-16 School, Sheffield

Perfect Partnership

I'm 436. He's 456. He's my partner in crime. The newest member of our group.
Our new order from The Eagle was to rob the biggest bank in the continent.
Step one: Fly overseas back to London. The Eagle was pleased with the fortunes we raided from our previous mission.
We arrived at the bank and headed straight for the vault. I picked up my 3 money bags and heard the click of a gun. I slowly turned around. 456 was on 1 knee, ring in 1 hand, gun in the other. He said those 4 inevitable words...

Ebony Armitage (13)
Hinde House 3-16 School, Sheffield

Pick A Flower

30, 29. Cold, I stagger towards the towering oak tree. 28, 27, 26. Red like roses and sweet like one, too. 25, 24, 23. The cherry blood travelled down my arm, tainting white daisies pink. 22, 21, 20, 19, 18, 17. Gripping my stomach. 16, 15, 14. The sinister tree scraped away flesh and attacked my skull. 13, 12, 11, 10, 9. My vision blurs. 8, 7. Flowers and vines are now colourful spots on the grass. 6, 5, 4. My body falls forward. 3. On the soft grass. 2. Rosemary and thyme. 1. Relaxes my bloody body.

Julie Eastwood Prince (13)
Hinde House 3-16 School, Sheffield

Countdown

I stand here looking at an app. I have 3 minutes left until I die...
When I was spending time with my friends they all said we should download the countdown app. What they didn't know was that the numbers on the app were when you were going to die. It said I had two hours left yet here I am writing this with only 3 minutes left.
They say a demon comes to get you when your time ends...
I'm only 11. I don't want to die.
If anyone wants to collect my body, I'm at 29 Brecon Crescent...

Amelia Maddison Trigg (11)
Hinde House 3-16 School, Sheffield

The Bank Robbery

12th October, 1995.
30 seconds left. The police are almost there. You need to hurry! The FBI is here. They are surrounding me. I am going to get caught. Help! Help, anyone! Can you hear me?
"Hi, Nooby, welcome to jail."
Suddenly I collapse. I hear shouting in my head. I'm dizzy. When I wake up, on my hand is the number 14. Then everything goes silent until someone speaks.
"You are safe. You are a special one."
Then everyone turns around... the game has started.

Esmond Thompson (11)
Hinde House 3-16 School, Sheffield

Ludo Star

And then there was 1... the last star I had to take out. I could do this. There were 3 out of 4 players out. All I had to do was roll a 3 to get it in or Number 13 would win. I could get that cash. Or else it was 10,000 down the drain. It was all on this roll. My hands were shaking out of fear and excitement. *Okay. Here goes nothing!* And there it was... I rolled a 2. My career in gambling was over. I was disappointed in myself. I was now poor and homeless.

Madina Yousaf (11)
Hinde House 3-16 School, Sheffield

The Horror Of The World

And then there was none.
Room 237 looked like a death room. All former life annihilated from the fabric of reality. The only sign that something had happened was the blood and gore that splattered the walls. Bodies lay strewn across the floor. What was once a small utopia now was no more. It was as if a god had flicked every horror movie in existence to every room except one. That didn't even express the horror. There was only 1 word that could. Hell.

Malachi Mason (12)
Hinde House 3-16 School, Sheffield

The Outside World

Day 237. My tests aren't going to plan. I have been in this villainous lab for too long now. It's time for my great escape. First, I need to check every room. As I check the rooms I make it to the last door: number 238. I check the room, it is empty. Perfect for my escape.
Day 238. After my tests with the others, I head for the room. I'm out. The green on the floor and the blue in the sky, it's... it's ineffable. But is it any better?

Riley Hague (11)
Hinde House 3-16 School, Sheffield

Within The Woods

It had been over 3 hours and she had not found anyone to help her yet. The dense army of trees loomed over her and despite it being a hot day, a menacingly icy-cold shiver crept up her spine. Night was starting to envelop the woods and she had still not found help. Her throat was sore, and she longed to suppress her hunger. The night sent a gentle breeze through the woods, wafting her face. Then, she saw 2 blue eyes peer from behind a tree...

Sophia Elizabeth Reed (12)
Ingleby Manor Free School & Sixth Form, Stockton On Tees

I Had 1 Heart

My story began on the 7th day of the 7th month.
I had 1 sister who ran in the woods with a silver bow shaped like a crescent moon.
I had 1 mother who was chased by monsters and my vengeful stepmother's ire.
I had 1 father, who glowered down from his storm-shrouded throne and refused to show favour to any 1 of his children.
I had 1000 siblings, who lived 1000 lifetimes. And each of the Immortal Ones could call themselves my kin.
But I had 1 heart, and through my own foolishness, I lost it forever.

Ellie Mack (17)
Kingsbridge Community College, Kingsbridge

Angel Numbers

111. She follows me everywhere. Following my every move. The ethereal being who watches over me, white wings protecting me from the bullets of the world. 111 the archangel only second to God. But 1 in the cruel hierarchy of pure ethereal beings such as themselves. Others have angels and archangels. Yet, I have her. The seraphim that keeps the devil's temptations at bay. And yet there was him. The only 1 guarded by the 1 that fell out of the cruel system. Lucifer the fallen angel...

Olivia Brzezinkska-Roberts (16)
Kingsbridge Community College, Kingsbridge

The Price Of Number 6

I am the 6th in line to the devil's throne. My brethren rule over me as the higher numbers. 1 brother is dying, so soon I shall be 5. But not without a high price. The price of rule, as soon as I am number 5, I have a timer. 6 years to get the throne, 6 people I need to kill, or I will fall.

Matthew Taylor (15)
Kingsbridge Community College, Kingsbridge

Eclipse

Hi, my name's Eclipse and I'm one of the 73 chaotic children that the devilish god Hades has. I know what you're thinking; wow, it must be so amazing being an all-powerful god, but it isn't. It just isn't! Lots of things have changed in the Underworld (and they really have changed) ever since your human technology came. Things have changed for the better.

It began on a murderous Saturday morning. All my siblings started devouring food like a pack of vicious, bloodthirsty wolves.

"Soooo, how did you sleep?" I said to my mom and dad, trying to make conversation...

Thomas Copping (12)
Moseley Park School, Bilston

Deals Of Chance

"Hey, chucklenuts! Yeah, that's right, you! Are you gonna bet or not?"
Only 30 seconds left to bet, and I was down to my last five pounds. The only question on my mind was... should I bet on a colour or number? Colour or number?
"I'll choose 13."
"Okay, but I bet 5 grand it won't be red. If it is, you have it all, deal?"
The wheel was spun...
The ball was let loose...
The roulette abruptly stopped...
Then the ball bounced from a black 26 to a red 13.
"How'd that happen?"
"They're all just deals of chance."

Dylan Chin (12)
Northampton Academy, Northampton

Agent 8

Kayla Smithy is a young girl who lives in central London. Her parents are currently away on a business trip to Sydney, Australia. Kayla is just a normal secondary student at Abbylane Secondary, well that's what others think of her as. Little do they know, she's a crime-fighting baddy in disguise. Known as 'Agent 8' by her boss, Kayla leads a double life. Since becoming London's 'superhero' Kayla's life has become difficult. A burden grows on her back after hearing tragic family news. People at her school worry about her every single day she is in the school building.

Ruby Peppiatt (12)
Northampton Academy, Northampton

Their Fading

2675. That's the number of my cell. A room stripped of effulgence. A room filled with just calamitous silence. A room where I, cellmate 101, was left alone.1459. That's the amount of days I've been left to rot, losing pieces of my sanity along the way. 35016. That's how many hours ago I last touched another living being. 2. That's how many minutes I have left until the nefarious guards come to end my life.
5. That's how many seconds the indignant-filled bullet took to reach me.
6. That's how many minutes it took death to selfishly take my life.

Widad Salaudeen (12)
Northampton Academy, Northampton

The Integers

Black and green scenery arose and a chill which felt like I was swimming across the Baltic Sea, engulfed my body. This wasn't like your average horrifying story with an eerie mist. No. 0s and 1s flooded everything and an ear-screeching scream bellowed through the vast land. Something felt off, a voice told me to explore but I was still trembling from the sight which turned everything melancholy. The digits reminded me of the code we did in computer science. Binary? I finally had enough courage to look around but then a fading light. A gateway formed. It was time...

Antal Csapko (13)
Northampton Academy, Northampton

Integer

Numbers, the greatest invention that we humans have ever made. They help us in the most complex calculations, some of the medium difficulty calculations such as 3(x - 3), and some of the easiest calculations such as 2+2 which as we know equals 4. From prime numbers to cube numbers and the Fibonacci sequence whose complexity is out of this world, which one is unable to fathom without a diagram. Binary in a computer as it is base-2 has its 1s and 0s. For example, 1011 would be 11. Without these numbers the world wouldn't be able to function.

Peter Ogundepo (13)
Northampton Academy, Northampton

497

Dear Diary, No. 497 here.
Today I starred in a maths equation! So did 3... as usual. They're always in all the maths equations.

Dear Diary, No. 3 here.
Today I starred in a bunch more maths equations, but everyone kept calling me annoying and odd. I wish I wasn't so famous.

Dear Diary, No. 497 here.
I haven't starred in any maths equations in over 2 weeks. No. 3 now has the record for most maths equations, even higher than 1!

Breaking news! 3 have been found dead. Suspect: No.497!

Belle Byles (12)
Northampton Academy, Northampton

Only 30 Seconds Left

I ran as fast as I could. Sparks flew everywhere. Smoke engulfed me. I climbed up a rusty half-broken ladder. I was met with a ticking bomb counting down. 30, 29, 28... I rushed and typed in the code my friend told me 'LMFB12'. The code was incorrect. Sweat trickled down my face as I typed another code. 'LMFBI2' incorrect. The timer counted down. 15, 14, 13... I had time for one more attempt. 'LMFB123' my heart was beating loudly like a drum. 'Correct' the screen flashed a green light in my face. I had done it.

Ben Richards (12)
Northampton Academy, Northampton

0 Chances

Maths test today, I only have one chance to pull it off. This test is so important to me, I would pull my 2 eyes out just to get the chance of a lifetime.
The time races past, 3 minutes until it starts.
4 deep breaths in, 4 deep breaths out. "Stay calm," I tell myself.
My 5 fingers shiver violently as I open the paper.
6 questions slap me in the face, hard.
I'm 7, 8, 9 seconds in. Numbers fill in my brain until it overflows.
I have 0 chances, 0 chances, 0-
"Are you... okay?"

Oyindamola Bagere (12)
Northampton Academy, Northampton

983

It was 3003. People were kept away and isolated. I was one of them. My number was 983. The rooms that they kept us in were plain and simple. We had nothing to keep us occupied. No phones. No TVs. Nothing. I was in my room that day. And I heard an indescribable annoying noise. I searched for it. Behind my empty bookcase, a small rectangular device-looking thing lit up. One thing I knew was that someone was calling. The number was odd. '983 calling' it read. I thought this was a lucky number for ages but I didn't know...

Megan Frost (13)
Northampton Academy, Northampton

Starting Anew

It starts on a snowy day, Santa is sick of the 9 elves who are playing tricks and not doing work. Santa immediately picks up the phone and exclaims, "I want these elves gone!" The elves gasp for air as they hear this shocking news. However, on the other side of the world, Grinch and Shrek decide to call Elfline, 0719695967. While the 9 elves are being shipped across the forest of candy canes, Grinch and Shrek are baking 22 delicious cookies. The new family joins together and eats 22 cookies and sings 2 albums!

Ava Pettit (12)

Northampton Academy, Northampton

The Orphans

The story of the orphans is strange; the place that the children live in is a minute cottage. Not a lot of children go there because it is a place on top of a very steep hill.
It was 7 o'clock in the morning when a little girl called Olivia woke up. She speedily got dressed and went down for breakfast but all of a sudden she heard Miss Trude yelling because somebody dropped their bowl and porridge bits landed on Miss Trude's shoes. Miss Trude was a very disrespectful person...

Rahma Djama (11)
Northampton Academy, Northampton

1945

It was 1945, many men wished death upon me. Blood in my eyes, I couldn't see. I was trying to be what I was destined to be. But soldiers were trying to take my life away. Suddenly, I got wounded by a German gunner and I couldn't look to the sky anymore. I screamed in agony, "Lord have mercy on me, have mercy on myself, don't let my heart turn cold!" My friend, a medic, rushed to support and quickly pulled out the first-aid kit. First I bled, then I was gushing...

Rijad Tula (12)
Northampton Academy, Northampton

When I Was...

When I was 8, my parents were brutally murdered.
When I was 9, I was forced to scavenge for food.
When I was 10, I became a thief.
When I was 11, I was unstoppable.
When I was 12, no amount of police officers could stop me.
When I was 13, I was nicknamed the Swift Stealer.
When I was 14, I had everything I wanted, but revenge.
When I was 15, I made it my life goal to seek revenge for my parents.
When I was 16, I had everything and more...

Max Knight (12)
Northampton Academy, Northampton

13 Years

Stuck. At the cold oak desk I've spent my life working at, I see the slow flakes of glittering snow fall as I look out my window, I think of him; it's been 13 years and I still think of him. Reaching out, I finally call him again. It rings and rings. No answer. He told me to call this number if I ever change my mind, maybe he is just busy. I get back to work, cold and draining. An hour later, it rings. I pick up the phone. It isn't him. They tell me he's gone...

Tyler Scrimshaw (13)
Northampton Academy, Northampton

24 Hours

1 hour left. I have been trapped in these 4 walls for 23 hours. 20 feet walls line the field as an ecosystem thrives around me. A large clock hangs in the air above me counting down the hours, I lie on the green grass below me waiting until I can leave. They put us here for population control. Roxon believed that there were too many children ruining our world, that they needed to get rid of us.
10... 9... 8... 7... 6... 5... 4... 3... 2...1...
Where am I?

Maisie Owen (13)
Northampton Academy, Northampton

Facing The Future Alone

I fell into a coma in 2022 from a car accident.
I slowly opened my eyes without seeing my family next to me. I asked about them...
"They're all dead."
How? I thought to myself.
"They died 11 years ago."
"What year is it?" I asked.
"3022."
I felt so dizzy that I could fall into a coma for another 1,000 years. I was wondering if this was a dream.

Vendija Graudina (13)
Northampton Academy, Northampton

2

Ruby was a normal girl, who wore her hair in a normal way, she wore normal clothes but... she lived in a very strange street! Every house was shaped like a number... Ruby lived at number 2 and her house was the shape of a 2... her fridge was the shape of a number 2... her bed was a number 2... her dog, Ruffas, was a number 2!

Lilly Hay (13)
Northampton Academy, Northampton

Colossal Party

It was 2099, the outlandish gargantuan world, the new metal environment, everything was made with metal, even humans. Wherever I gazed in this metal new robotic world I saw the gargantuan sky, colossal buildings and outlandish vibes. The danger of the past world was becoming slaves. The danger of the 2099 world is humans becoming robots. Technology went too far, no one can tell the difference between robot and human. The lackadaisical world went too far. The magnificent colourful environment became black and white. I was sitting in the middle of the enormous city thinking about my innocent life.

Aeman Hafiz Aslam (16)
Oldham Sixth Form College, Oldham

Addiction To Technology

It is 2099, I walk alone in the dark. I look around me, but no one notices me. It's like everyone has that urge to ignore everything, all they know is how to use a phone. You ask them questions and they will ask you to google your questions, it's like having a mind of technology controlled by them. It's wonderful how my parents didn't show me the unnoticed world.
It's okay to own technology, what is not okay is to be owned by technology. Smartphones are definitely smarter than us to be able to keep us addicted to them.

Karima Karima (16)
Oldham Sixth Form College, Oldham

15 Seconds...

"15, 14," said the lifeless mechanical voice.
I broke into a cold sweat. "Argh!" I screeched, my vocal cords scraping across my throat like nails on a chalkboard.
"12, 11," it continued again.
My head started to spin, my knees felt weak. I was now on the floor begging for mercy.
"7, 6..."
Again and again, my hands now wrapped around my knees, my body trembling.
"3, 2, 1."
Walls closed in, they came at me with immense speed, no time to think, my bones started to crunch, my skull cracked.
I knew all of this was because of *her*...

Florence Moore (12)
Priory Academy, Dunstable

Him

The call for my cake arrived - my 19th - I knew it had to come someday. I picked up, "Hello?"
The operator squeaked, "Hi, I'm calling for Livia Smith." He paused. "Is Miss Smith there?"
I spoke shakily, "Sorry, that's me." It was happening.
"Miss Smith, your cake's ready. There's also a note." He was oblivious.
"Yes, I'll come now, thanks." I hung up and got my coat. I wearily travelled to the bakery. I arrived, the same voice greeted me and handed me the cake. The cake read: 'Behind you - Tony'. His voice immediately came from behind.
"Hello there, Livia."

Meadow Dumpleton (11)
Priory Academy, Dunstable

Leap Of Faith

Time ticked, as the apprehensive girl was about to perform the most hazardous and unpredictable act of all time. Thousands of people joined in the crowd. Linda's heart was pumping out of her chest as she took 1 last deep breath. Without hesitation, she jumped. Closing her eyes, taking her mind off what was lying below, she counted the seconds till she had to grab the rope on the opposite side.
5...
Flipping in the air (the audience watched, mouths wide).
4...
Through the fire hoop.
3...
"I can do this."
2...
Gripping on for life.
1...
She reached out...

Doha Benmoussa (12)
Priory Academy, Dunstable

99p

I walked along the dilapidated aisles of a store which flashed its bright neon sign proclaiming, *Everything 99p or less.*
The price tags drowned me in cheap, repetitive, asinine horror of bright post-it notes mocking me with their cheap prices for flimsy short-lived products. They proclaimed 99p bread, 99p chicken, 99p Superman action figures, yet not a single note declared the one thing that I desired: the 99p aspirin amongst those endless shelves of budget, low-quality dread! The medical section only contained an old motherly lady asking if she could kiss it better for that accursed price, 99p!

Christopher Lim (13)
Priory Academy, Dunstable

Building V172

I was doomed. However, I didn't know that yet as I ambled along the pathway, trees swaying over the bare, moonlit pavements. It hadn't been far from here that my beloved grandmother had been buried. This town was shady. More than shady. According to my ancestors, the building known as V172 wasn't a place you desired to be. Nobody who had stepped over the threshold of that place had returned home to their families. Personally, I didn't believe in the supernatural. I didn't believe in ghosts, fairies. *So, why not?* I thought as I headed toward the entrance...

Keira Dolan (13)
Priory Academy, Dunstable

Room 131

It was Friday 31st October, Halloween. Unlucky for some.
I heard heavy footsteps outside my door. Suddenly, they came to a halt. When I'd signed into the hotel, I was told my room had inexplicable events recorded. Room 131 on floor 7. I silently listened, looking for anything 'out of place'. I only saw expensive furnishings.
Hours passed, there was a loud bang on the door. It was 3:11am. Who'd be knocking at this time? I walked to the door's peephole, I saw a spine-chilling figure. It was faceless, skin peeling. As I turned to run, it stood before me...

Ella Noble
Priory Academy, Dunstable

Room 123

The hallway lights flickered, my heart sank. I could only think of my mum screaming, *"Room 123, room 123!"*
Finally, I got there. I stood outside room 123 wondering if I should go home. I rang the bell, someone was there right? No answer. "Hello, let me in," I called. I twisted the door handle, it opened! I stepped in, slowly wandering around. OMG! My mum! She was dead on the floor! How? Why? I got on my knees and sobbed. I turned around. A man?
"Your mum isn't here anymore, are you next?" he said, smirking and getting closer...

Olivia Cleaver (12)
Priory Academy, Dunstable

The Camp

I looked down on my chest, the number 347. It was inked on my straw shirt. I was surrounded by people dressed just like me. "Hurry up," a voice beckoned as I was shoved back into reality.
"Where am I?" I didn't recognise my voice as it spilled out of my throat.
"You know exactly where you are, 347," the voice answered.
That number again, 347. I looked up and realised everyone was staring at me, mumbling to each other.
"Get back to work, 347." The tone of the voice had changed, irritated now.
Was I 347?

Lily Earles
Priory Academy, Dunstable

They Got There Before Me

29, the last number I put in for the safe code. My whole life depended on it. Did I get it right? Would I finally achieve this? It cracked open.
Inside was... nothing. *What happened?* I thought I'd predicted everything. No, they couldn't, they couldn't have got here before me, but the claw marks told me the opposite. But the safe was locked, how did they reach it? Of course...
He was with them as well, he must have used his powers. But there was no possibility he'd united with them... he wouldn't. Or would he?

Sophia Demchenko (12)
Priory Academy, Dunstable

A Normal Work Day

It was just like any other day at the Zadiv-6 research facility. Staff were going about their business, mechanical parts whirled and animated figures went about their day.
Max was busy shuffling through things in his new office, which was nothing more than a small space in front of a bunch of computers, perhaps in an attempt to get away from his sometimes annoying assistant, Cleo. He'd complained to his boss about him. The boss also wasn't happy about Cleo and fired him for not doing enough work for the last 6 months and disturbing others as per rule 26.

Mokshith Chahar
Priory Academy, Dunstable

Outbreak Perfected (Inspired By Integer 38)

"0038 has escaped from the Meta-verse, as every second passes by this robot is just roaming around," said the general. "This is too dangerous, put the city into lockdown, protocol 3.80."
After the announcement, all of the citizens rushed to their homes hoping that 0038 would not pounce on them. 0038 was nowhere to be seen where could it be?
The city was running out of supplies and the general was in his office, thinking what to do next. Then he heard, "Hello Mr Johnston." Then *bang*. Silence. 0038 was back...

Rishi Sakka (12)
Priory Academy, Dunstable

The Countdown

"5!" The booming voice made me jump. There was a man wearing an all-black suit. His face was completely blank.
"4!" The man shouted. I was sure I was on my own a minute ago. "3!"
"Why are you counting down?" I asked curiously.
"2!"
I wondered what would happen when he got to 1. "Hello? Can you hear me?"
"1!"
He then, in a much quieter voice said, "Ready or not, here I come!"
Slowly he turned to face me. My heart dropped as I saw what he was holding...

Imogen Morris (13)
Priory Academy, Dunstable

Number 13

I am number 13...
I gasped, trying to catch my breath back from the shock of where I was. I looked down at my wrist and I realised the number 13 was imprinted onto my wrist.
"13 and 7," I heard the muffled speaker say.
I panicked, trying to grasp a thought of what was going on.
I got picked up and taken to a room with metallic doors and punching bags, the doors revealed an extraordinary armoury in the room.
"You can only pick up 2 things."
We had to fight for our lives?
"3, 2, 1, *go!*"

Luca Paraschiv (12)
Priory Academy, Dunstable

Luton In Their First Champions League

I was happy, I was playing for Luton Town (in front of 81,044 fans) in the Champions League final. Real Madrid looked strong with Richard Hrok as striker and Calluski Wong on the left midfield but we, Luton town believe we can win this. I am in goal, Luton finished first in the Premier League and Connor Daniels was Luton's manager. The match started, Real Madrid did well in the first half then Luton came back in the second to draw level, the match went to penalties where I saved the final penalty and earned Luton's first Champions League trophy.

Quinn Kiely (12)
Priory Academy, Dunstable

Room 169

Bloody footsteps leading up toward room 169. Midnight on the dot. Screaming seems to appear from room 169 coming out from under the door. Stepping up towards the door the screaming seems to get louder and louder. Blood lies there on the door, spelling out 'help'.
My legs are shaking as I walk up towards the door. I turn the door handle getting scarlet-red blood on my hand. I walk in. Screaming appears from the bedroom.
Creeping up behind me, my dad appears. Me not knowing, he shoots me. Dead on the floor, still not knowing what happened today.

Phoebe Doyle (11)
Priory Academy, Dunstable

Never Look Alone

Room 237 was empty. I looked around, desperately looking for her, my best friend. It'd been 2 weeks since she went missing. My heart was racing and my hands were sweating. I didn't know what to do since this was the last room. *Bang!* A gunshot. I slowly walked out of room 237 as I felt my heart drop, then I found a note. I picked it up and read it out loud, "Turn around." I gasped as I saw her standing there with a sinister smile. All of a sudden, the lights went out. "Never look alone," someone whispered...

Natalie Chitescu (13)
Priory Academy, Dunstable

Ghostly Goings-On

Today I had visited my nan's house. Her house is surrounded by dead trees and plants. Also, her windows are dark, dirty and have moss growing on them. Furthermore, her house is filled with dust, cobwebs, creaking doors, ripped curtains and creaky floorboards. In addition, sometimes a voice will say, "22 is the number," but no one knows what that number symbolises. Everyone assumes that it's a ghost that lurks somewhere but no one has seen it before. Until... I went into the kitchen and could feel a gush of cold air hit my back...

Jack Rawlings (13)
Priory Academy, Dunstable

112 Courageously Saves The Day!

One night all the numbers up to 100 became non-existent. They were erased from every living being's memory. Even the lucky number 11! Which number could link to a human to save all the other numbers whilst the fantastical number 11 was gone?
Many years went by and just as every number was about to give up, number 112 (11's greatest enemy) courageously linked with the human number 11 was linked to before they all vanished. As a result of this, 112 saved the day.
What challenge will face these fearless numbers next?

James Pueschel (12)
Priory Academy, Dunstable

Prisoner 666

It was a dark stormy night. Roughly around 9:45pm, prisoner 666 was taking a shower then in the blink of an eye he pulled out a pocket knife. The prison guard fell motionless. Prisoner 666 sprinted out of the shower room into his chamber. He lifted up his mattress to reveal a hacksaw. He approached his iron bar window. *Clang!* A bar landed on the floor. An alarm set off. There was a police chase all night. Prisoner 666 had escaped the impossible. So I suggest you lock your doors tonight, there's a murderer loose...

Charlie Baxter (11)
Priory Academy, Dunstable

366

When I was a child my parents always said that if I was in a bad situation shout out the number 366. It was mine and my parents' special code. I'd never used it until this moment. We went caving for my birthday with my family, the most important people on the planet. We all split up trying to play hide-and-seek in the artificial cave when I saw the smallest crack with the best hiding space behind it, so, knowing myself, I squeezed my head just about through, but my neck was stuck. I shouted 366, would my parents come...?

Phoenix Burton
Priory Academy, Dunstable

The Jail Cell

The jail cell was open. I suddenly spotted the number 635 on the wall. After trying very hard, I found out what it meant. If I put the numbers all together it would give us a route. Me and my team followed it, keeping in mind he'd be tricking us. We found a board saying: 'Shimmer Hotel Room 635'. I went upstairs, I took my team with me, just in case. We walked up the stairs cautiously in complete silence. I went into the room, I couldn't find him. There was a note on the table... 'Can't catch me!'

Taashi Patel (11)
Priory Academy, Dunstable

Locked

It was locked. It wasn't going to be easy. There must be a code lying around somewhere. They checked the drawers again and found a piece of paper that had 8824 on. They typed the number in and the safe opened. They carefully took out a key that said 101. They needed to find the missing girl quickly. There was a hotel nearby named Sleep-Easy so they decided to check if there was a room 101. They found the room but the door wouldn't unlock. So they looked around some other rooms. They looked in room 104. There she was...

Niamh Osborne (11)
Priory Academy, Dunstable

World Cup 2022

A hot country like Qatar makes it hard for other teams to cope. Tears in fans' eyes and mixed emotions spread across the stadium. 32 teams have participated 16 will make it through. 8 will win out of the 16 left and 8 will qualify then 4, 2 and then there will be 1 winner from all 32 countries. The beautiful game of football all revolves around numbers. The amount of time, teams, shirt numbers, scores and the amount of people crowding around the world to witness what will happen and to see the 1 team who lifts the trophy.

Bobby Mcgrory
Priory Academy, Dunstable

To My Friend

The time was 20:55. Thomas was writing a letter to his best friend saying he was leaving for America, as he was writing he heard a clatter in the kitchen. "Who's there?" Thomas shouted.

No response.

Thomas sighed and got up from his seat and walked over. He looked in the kitchen and saw what seemed to be a cat-like animal but when it turned to look at him it was sheer horror. The creature seemed to have large sharp teeth then all of a sudden it lunged at him and he was engulfed in utter darkness...

Joshua Dunkley (13)
Priory Academy, Dunstable

10 Seconds Left...

There were 10 seconds left in the vault until the alarms went off. My assistant hacker was rushing me. I quickly grabbed the last bit of cash and ran out. Then he ran back out to the main floor and exited through the fire escape. There were SWAT vans and helicopters surrounding the casino and we went through the sewers to meet our escape car. We jumped speedily into the back. But as we left through the underground car park, the distant sound of bangs shocked us. We only had 10 seconds to escape... would we make it, or not?

Ben Middleton
Priory Academy, Dunstable

The Ferocious 15

They used to call us The Ferocious 15, known for our bravery and loyalty, until my so-called comrade-in-arms left me here to die. We were like brothers, but he betrayed me. Let me start at the beginning...
We were the 15 strongest Vikings on our deadliest mission yet; to take back our land. Unknown to me, my greatest ally was really a traitor. He made a deal with the enemy that on the 15th day he would lead us to their trap. One by one the Roman archers took us out, however their fate was worse, they let me live...

Rayyan Boksh (12)
Priory Academy, Dunstable

The Bomb

Suddenly a timer appears on the screen, displayed on it is the number 60:00. It starts ticking down. All of a sudden, a voice alarms me, he instructs me to go to the nearby shop. Therefore I decide to go.
When I arrive, I see people frightened and blood scattered everywhere. I start to observe what is happening and I see a bomb slowing ticking. In order to defuse the bomb, I would have to go through a dangerous obstacle course. But I don't keep focus and the bomb detonates. The whole city is wiped out by it.

Cameron Newman & Krystian Olszewski
Priory Academy, Dunstable

8's Time To Shine

This is 8, she is stuck in the warp of time. Every day she dreaded her time of day. Her biggest fear was messing up, this fear was not easy to avoid. All eyes were on 6 then 7 and at last her turn. 8 was usually children's worst nightmare (their bedtime). She would hear small children crying and begging for one more bedtime story. She would hear the parents protesting, and 8:30 is when there would be silence. However this amused 9. 8 didn't know why, but she knew there was a reason. But who knows? Only 9.

Nel Anna Plachciok (11)
Priory Academy, Dunstable

Heads Or Tails?

There is a chocolate left in the box and there are 2 of us, my brother and I. I choose heads and my brother chooses tails. I cross my fingers in hope of getting lucky. The penny is tossed into the air and we squint in hope of victory to taste the delicious bar of chocolate. We've agreed not to split it. And that might have been a mistake. I pray that I am the lucky one - don't fail me now. I stumble over to where the penny has fallen and...
"Shall we split it into 2 after all?"

Neve Janbey (11)
Priory Academy, Dunstable

Room 255

Suddenly I woke up randomly from what seemed like a nightmare but with no memory of it. I looked around, confused, I was in a dark empty room with nothing but a bed. There was two die... that together had rolled 13. The wind blew in a cold breeze.
I got up, something was scratching at the door. What was it? I covered my ears, and went back to bed. I ignored it. Because I couldn't go to sleep with the sound of scratching, I opened the door, but the sound didn't stop. It was coming from the broken window...

Keira Jay
Priory Academy, Dunstable

Number 6

Most people think that 6 is lucky, like when you play a game, but the Devil's number is 666. As brainless as I was, I dialled that number, not realising what I was doing.
Someone answered, but no one spoke. I hung up, but what I didn't notice was a circle forming around me... the floor was disappearing, little shards of it flying away. The ground sucked me up and swallowed me whole. Into the jaws of the Devil's lair I went, stuck, lost, alone.
Will I find my way out or am I stuck here forever...?

Rosie Cook (12)
Priory Academy, Dunstable

When I Turned 13...

Today was the day I turned 13. The day had been splendid until I stumbled across an odd scene, a murder. I had not anticipated this, though I had expected something bizarre today. It had shocked me at first, the corpse of the victim lying there with a gaping wound in their stomach. The murderer was just as surprised as I was. I stood there a moment, processing what I had just seen, being a witness to such a thing would obviously put me in danger, so I ran. Someone told me my 13th birthday would be special...

Mary Velea (12)
Priory Academy, Dunstable

The Unique Number 11

Number 11 was walking down the road. Even though he was the smallest 2-digit prime number in his circle of friends, which included 13, 23 and 31, this didn't bother him in the slightest for he knew that he was spiritual and very powerful. Whenever 11 was around good things happened. He was also the first rep-digit which meant he was the first number to be made up of the same number. Everything about him seemed lucky, he was also the 10th most popular number that people chose. But one day his powers ended...

Charlie Bates (12)
Priory Academy, Dunstable

Reflection

On a dark, gloomy night, a girl came across a broken-down house at the end of the road which was known as 11 Elm Street. Since 11 was her favourite number, she grew curious about what lurked inside the house, and so she walked in shakily through the door. To her surprise, she was welcomed by a large mirror at the end of a shadowy hallway. Slowly, she walked closer to the mirror and saw another figure standing behind her. Her heart dropped and she screamed as the door shut, forever imprisoning her in the house.

Lucas Maderazo (11)
Priory Academy, Dunstable

Night Terror

Bang.

There was a bang from downstairs, I checked my phone and the big bright screen read 2:54am. Stuffing my phone in my pocket, I crept out of bed to investigate the sound. Reaching the top of the stairs, I heard a phone ringing. I grabbed my phone to mute it, but my phone wasn't ringing. That's when I realised that I wasn't alone. Dashing back to my bedroom I hid under the bed. I grabbed my phone to call the police, the light from the phone illuminated someone lying next to me...

Sean Deardon (14)

Priory Academy, Dunstable

The Message

I froze in anticipation, hoping, praying that I'd make it out. The dice toppled over and landed on 3. I gasped with relief as I watched my piece move on its own, as if it was magic. On the table all around me I heard the screams of my fellow contestants before they all suddenly stopped. I jumped up from my chair and dashed out the door, I sighed with relief when I felt the sun's yellow rays cover me. A long ping came from my pocket and I grabbed my phone. My heart dropped as I saw the message...

Sophia Cook (13)
Priory Academy, Dunstable

The Mystery Door

I was on a late-night walk and I got lost and I needed help. I saw this 1 door that looked creepy. Number 21. I looked up and the door was massive. I was banging on the door and there were noises coming out the window so I walked away but when I walked away the door opened. I heard voices saying, "Come in." I was screaming for them to help me get home. I walked away but the voices followed me saying, "Number 21... Number 21."
I ran the fast as I could...
Then I woke up.

Jack Owen (12)
Priory Academy, Dunstable

Number 13

The number 13 is unlucky for some, But I never really understood why. It sits very happily between the numbers 12 and 14 without any problems at all, it's a prime number and the world would be a very sad place without it. The number 13 can be a great number! The baker's dozen means that you get 13 of an item, which means that the person gets one for themselves! I was born on the 13th which is just one of the many reasons why it is such an extremely great day for me and hopefully for you now!

Maya Patterson (12)
Priory Academy, Dunstable

16 Years Ago

It was 16 years ago today when I retired. I was the greatest criminal in the world. Life is supposed to feel good when you have everything in the world but my life felt empty. I felt unneeded.
So that brings us to now where I'm hanging from the vault ceiling in Fort Knox, my heart's pumping, this is what I was missing, the rush of robbing. There are 16 guards below me. I go to reach for my gas to knock them out.
Tink.
I knock the gas from my belt and it falls...

Stanley Morris (12)
Priory Academy, Dunstable

1943

1943, a world at war. I was a sniper on the Italian front. I had been scouting this village for weeks, my target was General Fritz Richter who was running a propaganda routine. Now I had just got back to the tower I was using as a vantage point when I saw a truck coming down the road, it would blow my cover soon! I grabbed my Springfield rifle and scope from the truck's fuel tank. I held my breath and fired, *boom!* The fuel tank exploded and took the truck and its occupants with it.

Sam Geddes (13)
Priory Academy, Dunstable

Only 30 Minutes Left!

Panic. Fear. Desperation. As I stand in line waiting to hear
the number 21, this is how I feel, hearing the siren, knowing
toxic gas is heading towards us. We inch forwards.
26 minutes to go.
My heart is racing, my palms are sweaty. Will we make it?
20 minutes to go.
I'm surrounded by worried faces. I can hear the plane
engines warming up, calling me with the sound of safety.
"Number 21, James, step forward!"
I've got it! My ticket to freedom. There is hope after all.

Ryley Warner (12)
Priory Academy, Dunstable

The Murder In 107

I heard a distant scream from room 107. I went to see what happened... number 10, dead on the floor. The window was open, the curtains flowing. I fell to my knees, 1 came running in, screaming for help, but no one came. Waterfalls were coming from my eyes. He asked me what happened. I couldn't answer. I went to see the cameras to see who it was. Camera 3, a black figure came and killed 10. It was a figure with the key. The only person who had a key to that room was 1. Was I next?

Sophia Collis
Priory Academy, Dunstable

I’m Number 87...

I was trapped, a number imprinted on my arm '87'. I wondered how it got there, I wondered how that happened. I was in a boxed room, yellow mouldy walls, water on the floor and rust on the ceilings. What was I wearing? Wet trousers that were torn at the bottom and a long-sleeved top that was torn by the collar bone. I looked at my arm again and the number was gone like it was never there or I'd never seen it with my own eyes. Suddenly, I froze as the door creaked open...

Ellie White (11)
Priory Academy, Dunstable

The Execution

I woke up in a white room with the number 46 tattooed on one of my wrists. I looked around and saw more people with numbers on their wrists. I went up to the person with number 32 and asked them what was going on. He said that due to overpopulation the government was eliminating people with low IQs. As he finished, a person wearing all black told number 1 to go up to the stage. As soon as he got there he got shot. Time was running out and I needed to figure out a way to escape...

Minudi Wellappuli (12)
Priory Academy, Dunstable

Alone

Where am I? I look down at a piece of paper - 11, what does it even mean? I look up and see a plain black room. There are no chairs, no tables, not even a window just emptiness. All there is is a door, it needs a 4-digit code. I put in 1234, it opens to the outside world. But nobody is there except some mutant creatures. I ask one where everyone is. It turns to look at me. I hear it whisper to me, "Humans went extinct almost 11 years ago. How are you still on Earth?"

Orlaith Keating (11)
Priory Academy, Dunstable

Lost And Found Again

13, my number is 13. I'd been stuck in an adoption home for 13 years, hence why my name is 13. I hoped to get adopted and today it came true. I was told to go to the adoption room. When I went in I saw a lovely couple sitting down. I thought, *yes*, immediately when I saw them for the first time. They asked how I felt about getting adopted and I said I was too excited to give them words. They adopted me and now I am having the time of my life with my new family.

Pari Patel (12)
Priory Academy, Dunstable

Saving Year 2099

Lio and I have time travelled to the year 2099 to stop a big disaster, where Earth will be turned into ashes. We need to stop the disaster, where a meteoroid will hit Earth. We need to make a weapon that will destroy the meteor. We have brought materials from the past to create the weapon. The meteor will hit the Earth at midnight, so we need to be ready.
We can see the meteor coming so we destroy it with a weapon. We travel back to our time after saving the Earth.

Anay Sagar (12)
Priory Academy, Dunstable

Frozen Winter

It was 2099 and no one was to be seen. I'd looked all over and hadn't seen a soul. I looked ahead and beyond but there was no one in my sight. All I could see was a frozen wasteland full of ice and snow. As the sun came out I started to look around for signs of life. I saw ice starting to melt from the ground. As I looked around I kept seeing life start rising as the clouds started to dissipate from the sky. A person started walking towards me in the distance...

Archie Lovett (13)
Priory Academy, Dunstable

24

I was number 24, alone and regretful, nobody was there to help me. I didn't know what I was up against and what I had signed up for. Being part of this was the biggest mistake of my life. I sat missing everyone that I knew and loved. I regretted every day I was there trapped, alone, cold. Suddenly, 1, 2, 3, 4 people came in where I used to be alone, people at last, after ages of being here I had people to talk to, people to get to know. What would happen now?

Chloe White (12)
Priory Academy, Dunstable

Run From Number 7

I am 7 that is my name... 7 is lucky... I am not. Everywhere I go... 7.
This has to be a nightmare.
No, it's gone on for too long. Need to escape. Running... not going anywhere. Help... someone please... door after door. 7, 7, 7.
Light... almost there... black. Floating around... cold... so cold. Must be death. Finally... free. No, too dark for death... falling.
Air rushing passed... then solid ground. No more 7.
Everything is normal... No an illusion... 7.

William Gibbs (12)
Priory Academy, Dunstable

The 6 Game

I was playing a game with my friends and I rolled a 6 and so I moved 6 but then the game ended and they went home. I went to sleep but then I woke up in a strange room with my ears ringing. Once my eyes focused all I saw was '6' all over the walls. I tried to move but I was chained to the wall and I saw something moving in the distance. It was my friends in red robes and candles floating around them. They said, "Too late," then it went dark...

Mollie Chapman (12)
Priory Academy, Dunstable

Counting Forever

3 years ago my life was much different from now. I eat less and I sleep less. This could be because I work late at a box factory. But nowadays I count everything from how many sips of tea I have or how many steps I take to get from place to place. Every day I try and beat my score, such as it took 2 minutes and 140 steps to get to work, now it takes 1 minute and 110 steps, I move faster and I count way too much. I think if I tried, I could count forever.

Bobby Ewers (12)
Priory Academy, Dunstable

The Dark Night

It was dark night on October 31st when my cousin took me to her massive castle-like house. The place was a haunted house located far away from populated areas and in the centre of the jungle. I saw tall shadows coming towards me, they stepped over me and disappeared behind the door. I felt a chill in my spine and gave a loud scream.
Then, my cousin was comforting me and I gave a sigh of relief and said, "Thank god, it was just a dream!"

Sidra Farooq (12)
Priory Academy, Dunstable

The 1st And The Last

Today was the day. I got in the car and went to the stadium to warm up for the game. I was told I was a sub.
30 minutes passed, the game had just started. 54 minutes in, I got subbed on. I was so nervous. I got 1 touch on the ball, the rush of the moment hit me and then *bang,* I got rammed into by the CB and my ankle snapped. I got rushed to the hospital and got the news I couldn't play football again. I was so devastated.

Callum Wilson (13)
Priory Academy, Dunstable

The Last Voyage

3 human lives in the hands of hundreds of equations developed over thousands of years yet who were millions of miles from Earth in a small, cramped aluminium tomb. Only sheet metal between them and death, only equations saving them from their natural state of non-existence, only numbers to help their helpless souls, numbers that the whole operation relied on; numbers lost in translation, through the vastness of space. Never reaching the brilliant minds of these 3 young astronauts in that space shuttle millions of miles away bee-lining to the surface, never to see their mothers, their children, their world.

Ethan Guatelli (15)
Robert Gordon's College, Aberdeen

When The Clock Strikes

It had been an eventful week. There were storms amongst storms, flocks of birds flying left to right and black cats prowling about everywhere. Crashing sounded. It was coming from downstairs.
I walked downstairs with a slow, timid step only to find the Grandfather clock had been shattered into a million pieces. To my surprise, it still worked, the clock struck twelve o'clock. The crashing grew louder but this time it was coming from outside.
I stepped out the front door. I didn't know where to look. Blood painted the pavement. Dead bodies piled high. The clock chimed once again.

Amy Reece (15)
Robert Gordon's College, Aberdeen

McChoices

The person stared with his mouth open at the large and colourful screen, bemused by an almost infinite number of options. You could have a burger filled with whatever you wanted (you could add or remove items). Their fries, small medium or large, were to die for. Barbecue sauce with chicken nuggets could allow you to be a child again. Ice cream, wraps, drinks, breakfast meals, kids' meals, a classic cheeseburger... This list was truly infinite and never-ending. At last his wife said to him, his eyes not blinking at all: "Have a Big Mac. You know you'll like it!"

Wali Moosa

Robert Gordon's College, Aberdeen

A Day Of Note

My hands are bleeding. The music exam is tonight. I have been sitting at my piano for 74 hours. No sleep for 3 days. This changes everything. Do I get into the music school? Is my career over? All I can do is pray.
I walk into the exam, my hands covered in plasters.
"C# scale, hands together, 3 octaves please," says the examiner. His monotone voice echoes through the hall.
I place my fourth and second fingers on the notes. This is the beginning of change. Suddenly my finger slips. I storm out the room. I'm over. I'll die.

Iona Crichton (15)
Robert Gordon's College, Aberdeen

7 Forever

There was a boy who was 7 forever. You might wonder if he ever moved out of his parents' house. He didn't. His parents grew old and weary. His dog had since passed away. His parents had aged 40 years since his 7th birthday. He hadn't aged once. His mates teased him for his high voice, his short stature, his light weight, his lack of strength. He hadn't been happy since his dog passed away. He began to contemplate his life, whether being 7 forever was worth it.
Then his dog returned. Maybe, 7-year-old Sam was happy again.

Toby Uzoh (15)
Robert Gordon's College, Aberdeen

Premature

My eyes burned. Blinding red light poured into my freshly opened eyes contrasting the cold chill sweeping across me. I finally regained my vision and looked at my unfamiliar surroundings. A frosty glass sheet lay in front of me. Beyond it, artificial lights poured over the room, decorating it in an unnatural red while engines hummed softly. I moved my shaking hand, not prepared to be used once more, and pushed open the glass door.
As I stepped out, my eyes found a screen on the wall. I gasped as I saw what it said. 21,346 years till landing.

Harrison Ellis
Robert Gordon's College, Aberdeen

Too Late

I swiftly glance down at my watch only to feel my heart plummet as I realise I only have 11 minutes to get to this job interview. My dream job, the opportunity of a lifetime, and I'm late. I feel my chest constrict with panic. The torrential rain clings to my glasses, obstructing my vision only adding to the stress. I glance left then right and take a long stride onto the road. I feel something crash into my side, knocking me to the floor. I collapse onto the pavement. Everything goes quiet.
I never made it to the interview.

Emma Barclay (15)
Robert Gordon's College, Aberdeen

834

She didn't flinch at all when the hot press made contact with the skin on her arm. Not a flinch. Number 834. Another way to dehumanise her. Some would see the helpless shell. Others, her eyes that raged with fire. Some would call it her fault. Others would defend. But they all had one thing in common. They all used her, all hated her. But most importantly they all underestimated her.
It was time for change and she had 834 reasons to fuel her burning hatred for them. 834 hours of captivity. But only 1 minute to change it all.

Isla Reid
Robert Gordon's College, Aberdeen

All The Time In The World

Of course I knew. Everyone knew. It was printed on every document - I had 13 days left to live. But then having lived 2197 weeks it seemed that I had lived life.
'You have all the time in the world'. We live by this motto day in and day out. It lies under every sign of our ruler. In reality you cannot say 'world' - who knows where we are actually living. Every book, every piece of historical evidence had been abandoned, burned.
13 days, 13 hours and 13 minutes left of life. I have all the time in the world.

Jessica Smith
Robert Gordon's College, Aberdeen

Elimination

"4 of you will be chosen. The rest will be eliminated," Captain says.
We all glance around at each other. 4 of us. That means that 6 will be eliminated.
"Follow me," he says.

We trudge down a dark corridor and what I see at the end leaves me stunned. An arena. Weapons line the walls. A thud sounds behind us as the door seals shut. And just like that, a spear whizzes past my head and I spring into action. My enemies are cut down around me until there are just 4 of us left standing. The chosen 4.

Toby Craik
Robert Gordon's College, Aberdeen

A Sinking Feeling

100 seconds to live. I was at the bottom of the ocean. It was cold, desolate and terrifying. 80 seconds left and I knew I had to fight back. I started kicking as hard as possible to free myself from my rocky prison. 60 seconds left. The air in my tank was running low. My breathing was laboured and my vision was blurry.
40 seconds left, I felt my foot break loose from the boulder it was trapped under. 20 seconds left, the only option was to pray I could make it out.
10 seconds left. I couldn't make it.

Michael Onyemeziem (15)
Robert Gordon's College, Aberdeen

Counting Down To Death

10. 9. 8. 7. 6. I'm nearly out of time. They're coming after me. I can hear the pounding of their footsteps. I can hear the slow drip, drip, drip of my crime following me like a ghost.
5. 4. 3. 2. They're getting closer. My heart is pounding in my chest. I can see my escape right in front of me. 1 more step. I reach my hand out in front of me, ignoring the vivid red stain that coats it like a curse, just as my world slips out from under me.
I'm too late. I'm dead. 0.

Saha Burnett (16)
Robert Gordon's College, Aberdeen

All 11

The church clock struck 11. There was a figure walking down the dark and gloomy alleyway in the town centre. The air was cold and you could see their breath in the surrounding air. He was dressed in a cloak. The person walked to the church, trying to remain hidden. They unlocked the door and slid in.
11 people had died. Me included. He was the murderer. He had killed me. My priest, the one who should be following God, broke a commandment. We were haunting him. All 11 of us, until he dies as we did.

Madison Murray (15)
Robert Gordon's College, Aberdeen

2

2s, all I can see is the number 2. One way in, one way out. I can't see. Why can't I see? I feel the harsh blistering wind penetrating my ears. I feel the air begin to disappear; I feel this life as I once knew it slipping out of reach. This burning sensation encloses my body. My mouth starts to burn. My eyes are lost to the endless darkness. Why am I here? Am I alive? My mind wanders into this vast eternal void, as my brain slowly sinks into the depths of despair. What am I going through?

Sam Binnie
Robert Gordon's College, Aberdeen

Time Waster

I peel open my eyes, oblivious to what the day will entail. I look up and I have 1 solemn day to live. One day! How could this happen to me? What am I supposed to do? I jump out of my bed in a panic, wondering what I should do with my last day on Earth. The thoughts are racing through my head. Hours pass by, I still haven't made up my mind, what am I going to do? Suddenly, my eyes shut; all I can see is white. I didn't even have the whole day. I wasted it.

Morven Begg
Robert Gordon's College, Aberdeen

5OLV3R

4 M15T3RY to some, just letters and numbers, but to me, my job. Numbers to rooms via padlocks. Numbers alone, boring. Letters and numbers though are an infinite code which I have mastered. This is the reason why I solve M15T3R13S (mysteries, in case you hadn't guessed). This is my life, full of codes and anagrams.
I love to watch cars for private registration plates, to try and unscramble their meaning. This is how I do it: 5-S, 4-A...
Yesterday, I saw one which said K1LL3R (killer) so, only joking, I called the police. That's when I got involved...

Freya Day (12)
Robert Smyth Academy, Market Harborough

Time To Sleep

02:51am. Her long black nails sank into my neck while another hand covered my mouth. I struggled, grabbing and gripping her hand. Struggling to push her over me, I looked around at the paint peeling off my walls. Dark grey curtains flapped in the open window. I glanced again at my clock. 02:42am. My hands, weak and shaking, helplessly gripped and grabbed at her long black hair, covering her pale white face. One last glance at my clock. 02:53am. Everything went black...
I jolted up sharply and glanced at my clock. 02:50am. My wardrobe door slowly creaked open...

Hannah-Chloe Balogun (12)
Robert Smyth Academy, Market Harborough

My Name Is 626

My name is 626. I am currently a 'dog' at an animal rescue centre. I came to Earth to cause trouble (not just because my spaceship landed here).
It's weird, you know, 'humans', they're odd-looking creatures. On my planet, there were no 'humans' who make you eat out of a bowl on the floor and sit on the floor and ruffle your fur around until you look like something that has been dragged through a hedge backwards.
But today a girl came in and her name was Lilo. To her, I am 'Stitch'. I like her. She seems nice.

Teigan Day (12)
Robert Smyth Academy, Market Harborough

Last One

It all went black. I was instantly knocked off my feet. When I eventually woke up everyone was gone! I looked around, no buildings, no animals, no nothing. I soon figured that I was one of the last people on Earth!
Having wandered around the now deserted planet, I was relieved to find somebody else lying around. There were 2 of us. Fires raged all around us and we had to accept our fate. No food, no water, it was only a matter of time before the human race would be wiped out. Humans and animals would be forever extinct!

Andrew Deathridge (12)
Robert Smyth Academy, Market Harborough

Me And Genocide

Bang! The gunshot added the next innocent up there. I was
7th in line, 7th to die, the 7th addition to the flood of blood.
I went further in the queue until I could see eye to eye with
the fire burning in his eyes.
I could hear a voice whispering in my ear, "Come on, you got
it. Just get it over and done with."
Oh, what to do? Who to trust? Where to go? But in the end,
we were both victims so I hesitantly walked towards the
tree, closed my eyes and waited.
"Tres, dos, uno!"

Melika Faraji (11)
Robert Smyth Academy, Market Harborough

Call For Help

I am an integer yet I am not whole. My name is 12. It all started when I woke up to excruciating pain, the number 12 was being drilled into my bone. I struggled against the tightly bound straps while I screamed, screamed into another number 12. She was mirroring me, almost copying me. I cried at her to stop. I closed my eyes to get away but she revealed fresh horrors to me that I shy away from. Please don't think of this as my story. Think of this as a cry for help. This is your final warning.

Alannah Fowkes (11)
Robert Smyth Academy, Market Harborough

Room 237

It was the year 2099 when my life changed because of hotel room 237. I had just checked in and took my bags up to my room. Then I left. I enjoyed the rest of the day.
Later that night I went back up to my room. Number 237 was haunted, legends said. I walked in with fear as a guest. I made myself a cup of tea when I realised my bags had gone missing. Room 237 was really haunted and legends were correct about it messing you up.
I went downstairs but they could only offer room 666.

Millie Swanson (11)
Robert Smyth Academy, Market Harborough

Binary Boy

110011001110, that's all I am, I could be words or pictures. But I'm just 1s and 0s. All I see is the simplified 11001001010010101010101111100011101 in endless rows and columns, encircling and controlling me, if I break free, do I lose, or do I win? I was once so much more, yet I don't remember anything. However, what remains is the lingering feeling that something is missing, as I gaze at the endless 1100100101001010101010101, I start seeing things, words, pictures, moments frozen in time for me to remember. But it is not me I'm seeing, it is someone else...

Tyler Marsden (11)
Scalby School, Newby

The Game

I rolled a perfect 20. The boys and I were spending a relaxing Saturday playing Dungeons and Dragons. We were rolling dice to determine damage on a particularly feisty dragon, when a wicked glint appeared in the Dungeon Master's eye. He opened an old, leather-bound book and began chanting. Me and the guys exchanged puzzled looks. After a while, our Dungeon Master stopped, looked at the 20 I had just rolled and yelled, "Intra." A bright blue face flashed before my eyes. I was my character, an elf. We were in the game, and there was a dragon above us...

Matthew Knowles (13)
Scalby School, Newby

2 People

My heart pounds as I find myself in a room that I do not recognise. Scattered throughout are simple tables and chairs, but none that seem familiar. Each table houses two people, one greying, one with a youthful complexion. 2 sides of life, an expectation to live, and outliving an expectation. 2 new people approach, placing water before me, and 1 before a young lady who I now see sitting across from me. She smiles, but despite her youth, she is plagued with wrinkles. So I must have the grey hair in our unfamiliar pair. "Mum, do you recognise me?"

Matilda Brown (16)
Scalby School, Newby

Room Number 3

Room number 3, on the third floor of the 3rd best-rated college in England, was said to be haunted. Students constantly reported strange sounds coming from it. Like floorboards creaking when there was nobody there and chilling, hoarse whispers concocting plans.
It had been out of bounds for years. Some say, that long ago someone was killed in that room and haunts it to this day. Non-believers say it's just the wind.
I was going to find out.
I walked up to the oak door and turned the rusty handle. The door creaked open, and there it was...

Abigail Marflitt (11)
Scalby School, Newby

Room 009

009? I'm no number, I'm a person. White walls, rock-hard floor, a small dingy bed. I take one last look and notice a big 'Room 009' pasted on the wall. I'm dressed in a hospital gown, am I in a mental hospital? I'm shaking, I look down at my arm, it's bleeding, and again '009' but this time blood is pouring out, not just some grey paint. Those monsters have clothed me in some horrible gown and now have carved a number into my hand. I'm caught off guard.
"009, 008, 007, 006 step out of your cells."

Jessica Kent (11)
Scalby School, Newby

Room 13

Room 13. A room that held death, sorrow and grief. Depression drenched the walls. The room cursed anyone who stepped onto the floor. The door, creaked, warning the innocent people of the horrors caged within the plagued walls, knowing it was too late for them already, a hostage to fate. It was a pit of misery, a prison, a hell hole. It was an ancient anchor of blood, rising by the minute. Neglect smothered the souls as they slowly faded. Room 13. A room that now held regret, guilt and corpses. Number 13, unlucky for some. Unlucky for my victims.

Lilia Banken (13)
Scalby School, Newby

I Am Number 1...

I woke up in an empty room, surrounding me were white walls. I lay on the dirty hospital bed staring at my wrist, *number 1? I'm not just a num-* My thoughts got cut off by a loud siren followed by a deep voice saying, "Number 3 has run away." I was confused but soon realised there were many rooms like mine, many people like me, just how many? "We are going to test your abilities," said the deep voice. *Abilities? What do they mean by abilities and what are they going to do to us...?*

Libby Marley (11)
Scalby School, Newby

The Mysterious Number

I was born with a peculiar number on the side of my sun-kissed neck. It read 10 and I never knew its true purpose. I just joined my brand-new school, hoping for a fresh start, hoping for new friends but all that came to a sudden end. It was a dark evening when I realised the meaning of the number...

Lilly and I stood at the clifftop, preparing to dive into the ocean below. We were naive and unaware of the dangers. I leapt, my head hitting a rock. Pain exploded everywhere. My blood embraced the ocean.

I awoke.

9...

Khloe Robinson (12)
Scalby School, Newby

The 4th Reich

I'm public enemy number 1. Me, the 4th Reich. Exiled to Saint Lucia for the rest of my life. The once-great Germany abolished. Gone. Let me explain...
I started as a lowly mayor of Berlin; then I retired and joined the German army and soon enough NATO and the EU fell, so the Government decided to.... well impose lots of new taxes then the people hired me, yes me, to deal with the Government so I led an armed revolution. I decided to bring back the Holy Roman Empire so mighty Germany would rise...

Reece Markham (12)
Scalby School, Newby

Number 63...

I woke up, my head swirling with fear. Then I saw it, number 63. It was on my wall, the ceiling, the floor. It was everywhere. I screamed. Nothing came out. Not a peep. I pinched myself to check whether I was in a dream or not. I wasn't. How was this possible, it wasn't surely? I lay there as if I was about to have a heart attack, as if the number 63 was about to jump out at me. Then I heard them, the words that tortured me, ''It's your time, the time you will become a number..."

Isabelle Templeman (11)
Scalby School, Newby

3 Minutes Left

The room was desolate, blank. On the wall there was a clock and on the small clock the number was shown. The number that would seal my fate. The number my life depended on, and it read 3 minutes. Thoughts ran through my head. I was trapped with 3 minutes to live. My life as I knew it gone.
Tick-tock.
My time was running out. 2 minutes. What was going on? Was this a dream? *Tick-tock*.
1 minute left until my fate was sealed. The end of my life was near. What could I do?

Layla Noble (11)
Scalby School, Newby

When Hell Broke Loose

I was only 5 when hell broke loose. A random fire almost destroyed my town. There were only 2 survivors - Derek and I. He is quiet... and weird. Whenever I mention going to a new village, he always stares horribly at me. With pleading eyes, I try to convince him to leave.
I go into his room and find him with a spell book, open at the page on how to set a fire. He turns and looks at me with a sinister look in his eyes. "You should not have walked in here. Now there will be only 1."

Florence Vickers (11)
Scalby School, Newby

Number 9

In my world, people are never described as numbers. They can be described as colours, seasons or just adjectives. But no, I see myself as a number, the number 9. A number with such meanings never discussed. It is a large number yet so young agewise. It may be an odd number, but I see myself odd too. Some people can be 9s and others can be 6s. Polar opposites. There is no problem with that. Even so, I believe I am the number 9. Wild, unordinary, maybe smart? I may be aged 15, but I am 9 at heart.

Jasmine Kaur (15)
Scalby School, Newby

Drop Dead

Guns were loaded. 5 dice were pushed towards me. I held them in my hand, the plastic warm against my sweaty palms. My first roll: 1, 1, 4, 5, 5. The 5s were removed from the quintet.
My score: 0. I rolled again this time it was: 5, 3, 4, 5. Again both 5s were removed from the set leaving only two dice remaining. My score was still 0. I rolled for the third time. This time 5 and 2.The unlucky numbers in this game.
My score: 0. The gun was held to my temple. I dropped dead.

Eleanor Nolan (13)
Scalby School, Newby

Subject 5

I wake up in a strange white room, it has pillows covering the walls, so I can't break out. In the middle of the room, where I am, there is a white bed, which has white sheets. The door is white with a number 5 on the door. The white alarm clock says 5:00. On my wrist is a number 5. The curtains are covered in the number 5. I kick the wooden door in and walk out of the door. I turn around and look down at a piece of the door. 'Subject 5'. I must be subject 5.

Cate Wallace (11)
Scalby School, Newby

First 5 Bite The Dust

My squad was obliterated by the impact of the tactical missile. I was the only known survivor.
The enemy command had been torturing me, physically and emotionally; although I knew my loyal squad would rescue me from this hostage hell.
We escaped, but the enemy had been alerted. They tracked us and sent a deadly air strike.
On my return, I reported to the president about the destruction of our vital marine base; he had no choice and uttered the words nobody wanted to hear. "Prepare the missiles!"
"They're ready."
He didn't hesitate to command, "Launch 5 at the enemy!"

Harry Sage (11)
Solefield School, Sevenoaks

11

It was my 11th birthday and I was about to be given the latest iPhone 14. Yes!
My devious plan had worked. I had deliberately smashed my old phone and had nagged and sobbed until my gullible parents had agreed to replace it. I excitedly opened the box and took out my precious new phone.
Dring! Dring!
Strange, a phone call already.
Confused, I answered.
"Happy 11th birthday, Ben," screeched a high-pitched voice.
The voice started to count the seconds; it reached 11 and cried, "Your time's run out!"
Bang!
With flames and foul-smelling metal, the phone exploded!

Ben O'Leary (11)
Solefield School, Sevenoaks

101

"Hello? Anyone? Where am I?"
I was in a pitch-black room. Warped shadows loomed over me with wailing cries. The room was infested with cobwebs and satanic spiders. Constant thudding from the walls was driving me insane and an eerie darkness was encasing my mind.
Flames spat out from narrow steel tubes. These flames were followed by an icy wind. My teeth were chattering, and before I knew it, I was in the corner trembling and manically sobbing. Large rodents bit into my shins - their teeth like flick-knives.
My brain clicked: I was in 101 - Room 101...

Henry Nikolich (11)
Solefield School, Sevenoaks

999

A car was following me. I sped along the dark motorway, heading home after a stressful day; lights of oncoming cars adding to my tension. There it was again, right up my bumper. I pulled over. So did the other car.
A shady figure stepped out. Although it was night, he wore dark glasses and was dressed entirely in black. A skull tattoo on his hand glimmered under the lights.
Breathing hard, I tried to run, but my legs were magnetised to the ground. My heart stopped. A surge of pain. I fell.
"999! Come quick. Fatality at the roadside."

Kasten Grol (11)
Solefield School, Sevenoaks

4368

4368, the number of my nightmares. That number haunts me, penetrating my dreams. The dull orange jumpsuit reads: 4368.
I've never forgotten the day I lost my him. I hate my spawn-of-Satan-like stepmother - clever and controlling - she will never let me visit him. I plead to go to see him and have one more conversation.
"You're not allowed to do that. He still has 217 days left to serve."
But, in 31 weeks, Dad and I will plot our sweet revenge on the lawyer, my stepmother, the reason my father is prisoner number 4368.

Charlie Evans (12)
Solefield School, Sevenoaks

The Game Of Dice

I had been sick, about to die. He had saved me, but at a price.
He was calling in his debt for my wagered years of youth and health. It was a game I had to win.
Under the cold, fluorescent moon, I kissed the dice held in my cupped hands. *Angels be by my side,* I prayed. Hideously, his eyes turned a tinted luminescent shade of green as he grinned with menace. "Let's play."
Flexing his long, pale fingers, he picked up the dice from my trembling palm and rolled a 9.
My hand shook. I rolled an 8...

Dexter Buhmann (12)
Solefield School, Sevenoaks

Only 30 Seconds Left!

Boom! The countdown has begun. I only have 30 seconds left to get out of here!
With Van Gogh's Sunflower painting under my arm, I need to get to the car in time before the bomb blows. I've placed a deadly detonator! As I fill my bag, in the distance, I can hear the screeching of tyres turning a corner! Time is running out... 15... 14... 13... before the explosion comes to life and flames as big as trees devour the building. As I get into the car, there are only 5... 4... 3... seconds left, but where's the painting?

Aaron Wrafter (11)
Solefield School, Sevenoaks

Agents

It was nightfall; my time. I was waiting in my room for the signal. The task - eliminate enemy Agent Yeltsin.
Like a shadow, I approached - surprisingly, his window was open. Clambering through it, I saw two guards in front of me. I shot first and they both fell dead, I looked around. Nothing.
Opening the door to his office, I noticed a file, a computer and a gun. Curious, I opened the file and scanned the sheet. Detailed instructions on how to find and kill Agent 76.
I am Agent 76!
As I struggled to understand, the door burst open...

Lewis Stanley (12)
Solefield School, Sevenoaks

Doomed

I'm doomed.
Although I am innocent, I can see nothing but gloom ahead.
My life is folding inwards like a scrapyard vehicle in a car crusher.
My bad luck started when I discovered my nephew was in hospital - a tag on his toe - due to poisoning. The sergeant in charge swelled with pride when he found the poison in my cupboard - and grinned even more when he found proof of its purchase in my credit card records.
But it wasn't me.
And there's no way to prove it.
Here I am, wrongly imprisoned in cell number... 13.

Oliver Bayliss (11)
Solefield School, Sevenoaks

Wall Street Crash

Numbers. The script of the modern world. Every day, numbers function as the code used everywhere to show and transfer information.
Another way the number is used is in banking. Especially in the stocks.
A young lady named Hannah sits in her office, looking from her penthouse view at the Wall Street stock market. She smiles, feeling on top of the world. But then, her whole life changes in seconds. She sees on a screen in her office that the value of the stocks has plummeted.
She gets up without hesitation, strolls onto the balcony, and jumps to her demise.

Joshua Aisthorpe-Buckley (12)
The Henry Beaufort School, Harestock

Room 237

Room 237 was empty. Plastered walls towered above me as my feet sank lower and lower into the ground. We had been promised an answer but left unsatisfied. Maisy was so far out of sight. I could already imagine the downhearted cry of her mother when we revealed this recent tragedy. Scanning the room just produced more despair as the beige walls stood in complete stillness. No evidence, no proof, no lead. Whatever path we were following had been swept away by the wind, leaving us where we started with 2 sorrowful parents and a case of a missing girl.

Saski Michael (13)
The Henry Beaufort School, Harestock

The Dice

I woke up in my bed, I looked down at the floor and found my slippers. On the floor, I found a dice, on the number 6. When I looked at it, I noticed that the room was becoming bigger and bigger. The more I looked at it, the more the room started to change, I was shrinking, smaller and smaller. It was hard to know what was happening, or why. I found myself back in my bed, but awake. The dice was no longer there, it had disappeared. Was it all a nightmare?

Elliot Prince (15)

Values Academy, Stockingford

Why The 6... Why?

I rolled the dice, the room went silent. "Please not a 6, anything but a 6." I leaned forwards and to my horror, it was a 6. I looked up at the shocked faces of the people playing this sick and twisted game. They were not shocked, not one bit, they were happy I rolled a 6. I picked up my piece, ready to accept my fate when one of the people playing this so-called game grabbed my arm. "It was fun playing with you."

Jack Goodman (15)
Values Academy, Stockingford

The Vase

"Jack wins again! 57-23 points."
How I win by the same amount of points every time has always been a mystery for others. People say I cheat, but they don't know. They don't know about the vase. This vase is said to let you win at any game you play. This is more of a curse than anything. When I found it, the time was 00:57. I did not know about its powers until after I took it. I win, but everyone accuses me of cheating, judging and laughing at me for winning with 57 points every time.

Muhammad Shuayb Eradhun (14)
Wandsworth Hospital And Home Tuition PRU, London

YOUNG WRITERS INFORMATION

We hope you have enjoyed reading this book – and that you will continue to in the coming years.

If you're the parent or family member of an enthusiastic poet or story writer, do visit our website **www.youngwriters.co.uk/subscribe** and sign up to receive news, competitions, writing challenges and tips, activities and much, much more! There's lots to keep budding writers motivated!

If you would like to order further copies of this book, or any of our other titles, then please give us a call or order via your online account.

Young Writers
Remus House
Coltsfoot Drive
Peterborough
PE2 9BF
(01733) 890066
info@youngwriters.co.uk

Join in the conversation!
Tips, news, giveaways and much more!

Scan me to watch the Integer video!